WOMEN'S PRO BASKETBALL TODAY

THE HISTORY OF THE NEW YORK

LIBERTY

Published by Creative Education
123 South Broad Street, Mankato, Minnesota 56001
Creative Education is an imprint of The Creative Company

Design by Stephanie Blumenthal
Cover design by Kathy Petelinsek
Production design by Andy Rustad

Photos by: NBA Photos

Library of Congress Cataloging-in-Publication Data

Frisch, Aaron, 1975-
The History of the New York Liberty/ by Aaron Frisch
p. cm. — (Women's Pro Basketball Today)
Summary: describes the history of the New York Liberty professional women's basketball team
and profiles some of their leading players.
ISBN 1-58341-011-2

1. New York Liberty (Basketball team) Juvenile literature. 2. Basketball for women—United States
Juvenile literature. [1. New York Liberty (Basketball team) 2. Women basketball players
3. Basketball players.] I. Title. II. Series.

GV885.52.N44F75 1999
796.323'64'097471—dc21
99-18889
CIP

First Edition

2 4 6 8 9 7 5 3 1

Since 1886, the stately Statue of Liberty has stood tall in New York Harbor, welcoming immigrants and returning natives alike to the freedom of America. It was only appropriate, then, that one of the first Women's National Basketball Association teams should be the New York Liberty, represented by a logo of the massive statue. After all, it was the WNBA that finally brought foreign basketball talents and American stars playing abroad to the United States to create a well-grounded league of their own. In their two seasons, the Liberty have become a league power, driven by defensive demon Teresa Weatherspoon, smooth scorer Sophia Witherspoon, and a balanced roster of gritty talent. It is this New York collection of athletes that has raised a new torch in the East.

COQUESE WASHINGTON

(ABOVE); KISHA

FORD (BELOW)

B-BALL IN THE BIG APPLE

In late 1996, when the newly formed WNBA scoured the United States for host cities for the eight charter-member teams, a dream decades in the making was about to be realized. For years, outstanding female basketball players had longed to play in American arenas in front of American fans. All attempts to create lasting women's leagues in the U.S., however, had failed, forcing athletes to take their talents overseas.

As American players prepared to return home and foreign players packed their bags for the United States, the WNBA settled on cities for its fledgling teams. It was only natural that one of the cities chosen was New York City, the largest metropolis in America. To build a strong and knowledgeable front office, team president Ernie Grunfeld—who also heads the New York Knicks—quickly hired Carol Blazejowski as vice president and general manager.

Blazejowski brought an outstanding basketball background to New York. As a one-time College Player of the Year, the three-time All-American forward had an eye for talent and a knack for winning. And as a former marketing executive for Adidas, Blazejowski brought considerable business savvy to the franchise. New York basketball fans also took it as a good omen that the general manager once scored an all-time record 52 points in Madison

PLAYMAKER TERESA WEATHERSPOON

HEAD COACH NANCY

DARSCH (ABOVE); '98

ROOKIE GUARD NADINE

DOMOND (BELOW)

Square Garden, the "World's Most Famous Arena" that the new women's team would call home.

New Yorkers soon learned the name of their new team: the Liberty, in homage of the majestic statue that stands in the city's bay. To head the charge of the Liberty, New York management brought east an outstanding collegiate coach from the Midwest: Nancy Darsch.

Few could question Darsch's credentials as a coach, having led Ohio State to a 234–125 record and four Big Ten Conference championships over a 12-year stretch. The coach also promised to instill a defensive style of play not unlike that of New York's beloved Knicks. With the biggest women's league in history about to take center stage in the fabled Madison Square Garden, the anticipation began to build.

THE TWO SPOONS

Because of the WNBA's short preseason, players coming together from around the world to form teams had little time to develop team chemistry before the regular season. Liberty management knew that its new team would need both experience and defensive intensity to compensate for the short training camp. Fortunately, New York would soon have two players that definitely fit the bill. The first arrived on January 22, 1997, when the league assigned point guard Teresa Weatherspoon to the Liberty.

In addition to outstanding playmaking ability and defensive skills, Weatherspoon brought unparalleled toughness, tenacity, and enthusiasm to New York. Weatherspoon's rise to the WNBA is a storied one. Growing up in Pineland, Texas—a town of 862 people—Weatherspoon played sandlot ball with the town boys. To compete against her taller opponents, she was forced to develop a strong defensive game and excellent ball-handling skills.

In the early 1980s, Coach Leon Barmore recruited Weatherspoon to Louisiana Tech, where she led the school to the 1988 national championship, earned the Wade Trophy, and shattered the school records in steals and assists. "In all my years, I never met an athlete who works so hard at practice," Barmore said. "She practiced every day like it was her last, and that's what made her so tough. . . ."

After college, "T-Spoon" or "Spoon"—as she is known—played abroad for years in front of crowds of only a few hundred fans. From there, the outgoing small-town girl made a fluent transition to New York and the legendary Madison Square Garden. The city and player immediately fell for each other. Blazejowski knew that New York had an instant star. "She may be the best guard who has ever played this game," the general manager said.

TEAM SCORING LEADER SOPHIA WITHERSPOON (ABOVE); VETERAN CENTER KYM HAMPTON (BELOW)

REBECCA LOBO ENJOYED A 100-GAME WIN STREAK

Although the fiery Weatherspoon would be the glue that held the first-year Liberty squad together, the scoring punch would come from another "Spoon" drafted three months later: 5-foot-10 guard Sophia Witherspoon. After the little-known guard from Florida slipped to the second round of the WNBA Draft, Blazejowski eagerly snapped her up. "Sophie has always been one of my favorite players," the general manager said. "She does a lot of things. Everyone talks about her outside shooting ability—her scoring ability—but she's quick as a cat, has terrific hands, and plays terrific defense."

The differences between the backcourt teammates were striking: one was a talkative sparkplug known for her defensive tenacity, while the other was a soft-spoken sniper with a fluid jump shot and underrated defensive skills. It would not take long, however, for Liberty fans to find that they had a fast-rising star in Witherspoon. The New York faithful soon nicknamed the versatile shooting guard "Serving Spoon" and waved spoons in the stands to honor the backcourt duo.

"Some people classify Spoon [Weatherspoon] and me as a Stockton and Malone," Witherspoon said, referring to the famed Utah Jazz duo. "It's a great honor, especially with Spoon, who brings a lot to the team—a winning attitude, experience, aggressiveness. She hates to lose, and that rubs off on us."

FORWARD TRENA TRICE (ABOVE); OFFENSIVE THREAT KISHA FORD (BELOW)

NAME: Teresa Weatherspoon

BORN: December 8, 1965 (Jasper, Texas)

POSITION: Guard

HEIGHT: 5-foot-8

COLLEGE: Louisiana Tech '88

AWARDS AND HONORS: Two-time All-WNBA Second Team, two-time WNBA Defensive Player of the Year, WNBA Player of the Week 7/26/98

One of two players originally signed to New York, Weatherspoon has proven herself to be a defensive force in the league without missing a start. In 1997 she led the WNBA in assists and steals, including a 12-assist performance on August 20th. In 1998 she continued her impressive numbers, finishing first in steals and second in assists.

STATISTICS: 363 career assists

Year	Average	Average Assists	Avg. Steals
1997	7	6.1	3.04
1998	6.8	6.4	3.33

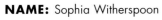

NAME: Sophia Witherspoon

BORN: July 6, 1969 (Fort Pierce, FL)

POSITION: Guard/Forward

HEIGHT: 5-foot-10

COLLEGE: Florida '91

AWARDS AND HONORS: WNBA Player of the Week 7-6-97

Witherspoon proved to be a steal in the second round of the general draft in 1997. That same year, she led the Liberty in three-point shots made and attempted, including a season-high 27 points against L.A. on August 20th. Witherspoon spent the offseason playing professional ball in Turkey before maintaining her numbers in the WNBA for a second season, finishing 12th in league scoring average.

STATISTICS: 820 career points

Year	Average	Total Points	Avg. Rebounds
1997	14.5	407	3.0
1998	13.8	413	3.0

PORTRAIT

SOME SEASONED DEFENSE

Even before the Liberty added Sophia Witherspoon, the WNBA assigned 23-year-old forward Rebecca Lobo to the roster. At 6-foot-4 and extremely athletic, the tenacious rebounder was one of the best-known collegiate players in America in the 1990s. As a senior at the University of Connecticut in 1995, Lobo won virtually every individual award given at the collegiate level, including the Wade Trophy as the nation's top women's player.

But more important to the star forward was UConn's perfect 35–0 season and the national championship. After bringing home the trophy and earning Final Four Most Valuable Player honors, Lobo joined the U.S. Women's Olympics Team for a world-wide tour. The tour, capped by a gold medal in the 1996 Olympic Games, ended with a 60–0 record, giving Lobo a personal winning streak of 95 games—one of the most remarkable streaks in basket-ball history.

PHYSICAL FORCE KYM HAMPTON

With Lobo and the two Spoons forming the team's nucleus, New York drafted the players that would become the original Liberty team. On February 27, the team assured itself a formidable center-forward tandem by drafting 12-year veteran Kym Hampton and 26-year-old Vickie Johnson.

At a powerful 6-foot-2, Hampton brought a physical game and outstanding rebounding skills to New York. The three-time high school state shot-put champion, who ranks ninth all-time among NCAA rebounding leaders, is also a musical talent who often belts out the national anthem before Liberty games. Johnson, a two-time collegiate All-American, complemented Hampton's power approach perfectly with a finely tuned offensive game.

The Liberty roster was rounded out two months later with the addition of three more players. Veteran Sue Wicks, a 6-foot-3 forward, was drafted to solidify New York's bench support. The move also represented a dream come true for Wicks, who had always longed to play at Madison Square Garden. "The veteran players on this team don't want to be stars anymore," she said, summarizing the players' happiness to finally have a prominent American league. "We just want to win. We've all been holding out as long as we could to go out winners in this sport."

Trena Trice, a 6-foot-2 forward, also brought veteran experience, along with a knack for scoring. Trice once scored 51 points

in one game—still a Spanish League record. The Liberty added some youthful energy to the veteran mix by acquiring 22-year-old guard Kisha Ford, who entered the professional ranks after setting Georgia Tech's all-time career scoring record with 1,955 points.

Completing the Liberty roster was Rhonda Blades, a hard-nosed guard who earned a spot through an impressive try-out performance. With a combined 48 years of experience among the players and a defense-oriented mentality, Blazejowski had at last assembled a team ready for the Big Apple. "There's pressure here to be the best," she said. "But we have an intense, spirited bunch. . . ."

A RISING IN THE EAST

History was made on June 21, 1997, when 14,284 fans packed into the Great Western Forum in Inglewood, California, to witness the WNBA's first regular-season game. Although the jittery Liberty, playing in front of a national television audience, started slowly, seasoned veteran Trena Trice ripped off six early

GUARD RHONDA BLADES

(ABOVE); 6-FOOT-3

FORWARD SUE WICKS

(BELOW)

17

points to boost New York to a lead over the Los Angeles Sparks. New York would never surrender the advantage, fending off the Sparks for a 67–57 win.

The victory was a vivid demonstration of the balanced teamwork that would become a New York trademark. While spark-plug guard Teresa Weatherspoon handed out 10 assists and Rebecca Lobo paced the Liberty with 16 points, frontcourt mates Vickie Johnson and Kym Hampton each put 13 points on the board. "With this team," guard Sophia Witherspoon said, "it can be anybody on any night. You can't focus on any one person."

After beating the Sacramento Monarchs for its second win, New York continued to roll, beating the fierce Houston Comets—who would soon prove to be one of the league's strongest teams—three times within the next 10 days. New York's 70–67 win over Houston on July 2 pushed the Liberty to 5–0 and Lobo's amazing personal streak to an even 100 games. "Someone is going to have to play near-perfect to beat this team," said coach Denise Taylor after her Utah Starzz fell to the Liberty. "They're not invincible, but close."

Both winning streaks and the sense of invincibility, however, came to an abrupt end five nights later. Behind a 45–27 second-half surge, the Phoenix Mercury gave New York its first taste of defeat, snapping the Liberty's streak at 7 and Lobo's at 102.

Darsch's squad quickly found the winning track again, going on a five-win tear and crushing its opponents by an average of 14 points a game. The Liberty's smothering defense and

balanced offensive attack pushed New York to a league-best 12–2 mark. In the streak's capping victory, Liberty guard Rhonda Blades rocked the L.A. Sparks with a flurry of first-half scores, and Witherspoon finished them off with a 24-point explosion.

Unfortunately for New York fans, the Liberty's torch seemed to go out as they went a mere 4–9 in their next 13 games. The high-flying Lobo and workhorse Hampton finally led the Liberty back into the win column with a 79–72 overtime victory over Cleveland on August 24. After roaring out to a 17–2 lead to start the game, the Liberty hung on to snap a four-game skid. "I don't know what it would have done to us to have another loss today," Darsch said with relief. "We had to have this win."

After making it into the playoffs, New York faced a stiff challenge in the Phoenix Mercury and their star Jennifer Gillom, who had torched the Liberty for an average of 18.5 points and 10 boards in the teams' four regular-season meetings. In the WNBA semifinals, however, New York took its stingy defense to a new level, allowing a league record-low 41 points in a 59–41 blowout victory. Lobo and Hampton were again unstoppable, combining for 30 points and 23 rebounds and helping hold Gillom to a mere nine points.

Two nights later, the Liberty took the floor to vie for the first WNBA crown with Cynthia Cooper—the league scoring champion and MVP—and her Houston Comets. Although the Liberty had beaten the Comets in three of four regular-season contests, Houston rode Cooper's 25 points and a stifling defense of its own to a 65–51 win and the league championship. "It's a very painful loss for us," said Weatherspoon, "but at the same time, we really have to be positive about a lot of things that we've done. . . ."

PORTRAIT

NAME: Rebecca Lobo

BORN: October 6, 1973 (Hartford, CT)

POSITION: Center/Forward

HEIGHT: 6-foot-4

AWARDS AND HONORS: 1997 All-WNBA Second Team

Originally assigned to the Liberty with Teresa Weatherspoon, Lobo led the team in blocked shots and rebounds in 1997, finishing in the league top five in both categories. Her season-best performance of 27 points, 9 rebounds, and 5 blocked shots came against Utah on August 19th. The following season, Lobo's numbers dropped slightly, though she remained in the league top 10 in rebounds and blocks.

STATISTICS: 698 career points

Year	Average	Total Points	Avg. Rebounds
1997	12.4	348	7.3
1998	11.7	350	6.9

NAME: Nancy Darsch

BORN: December 29, 1951

POSITION: Head Coach

SEASONS COACHED: 1997-98

RECORD: 36-24

Nancy Darsch led Ohio State to four Big Ten Championships and seven NCAA appearances in 12 seasons before joining the WNBA. In addition, she served as assistant coach on two Olympic gold medal-winning squads. Darsch led the Liberty to a 17-11 WNBA runner-up finish in 1997. Her team's record was second-best in the league and included a seven-game winning streak in late June. The Liberty defeated the Phoenix Mercury in the first round of the playoffs before falling 65-51 to Houston in the championship. The following season proved to be a disappointment for Darsch and the Liberty, who finished 18-12 but narrowly missed the playoffs with crucial losses in the season's final two games. Darsch was released at the end of the season and hired to helm the struggling Washington Mystics.

PORTRAIT

23

The tenacious Weatherspoon, who led the league in steals with an average of three per game, was named the WNBA Defensive Player of the Year and—along with Lobo—earned All-WNBA Second-Team honors. Witherspoon finished among the league's scoring leaders with a 14.5 points-per-game average and nailed a remarkable 44 three-pointers during the season. Johnson and Hampton, who formed a reliable one-two punch at forward and center, combined for nearly 20 points and 10 boards per game. Yet despite the solid numbers, New York was left empty-handed to dream about next year.

ON THE ROAD AGAIN

After dwelling on the disappointing conclusion to an otherwise fantastic first season, the Liberty players reported to training camp in May 1998 for another run at the title. With its central core of stars returning, many fans and experts had high expectations for New York.

Although the Liberty lost backup guard Rhonda Blades through the WNBA's Expansion Draft, they also acquired some free-agent bench support. Two of New York's most notable additions were guard Coquese Washington and center Elisabeth Cebrian. Washington, a defensive specialist, joined the team after setting a Notre Dame school record with 307 career steals. Cebrian—a 6-foot-5 center known as the "Gigante Feminino," or "Giant Woman," in Spain—led the Spanish League in rebounds in 1997 and 1998 and was named league MVP each season.

With a five-game road trip to open the 1998 season, the Liberty knew that the going would not be easy. This point was driven home with a season-opening loss to the Cleveland Rockers, who squelched any chances of a repeat of New York's fast start in 1997.

SPANISH STANDOUT

ELISABETH CEBRIAN

(ABOVE); NADINE

DOMOND (BELOW)

Two more losses followed before New York finally crushed the Sacramento Monarchs for its first win. A Witherspoon layup late in the first half triggered an 11–0 run capped by reserve forward Albena Branzova's 15-foot jumper. New York's lead ballooned to 25 before the horn sounded on a 64–48 win. "We made a few adjustments offensively, but mostly we had to make an adjustment in our intensity and attitude," Rebecca Lobo said, explaining the difference in the win.

The Liberty lost the next night but then went on a tear, winning four straight games at the Garden. In the fourth win, a 71–68 victory over Phoenix, Vickie Johnson and the two Spoons turned into a three-headed monster; Johnson and Witherspoon each burned the Mercury for 23 points, while the 5-foot-8 Weatherspoon cleaned the glass with 10 rebounds.

Eight nights later, the red-hot Detroit Shock—winners of their last six games—came into Madison Square Garden and left with a broken streak. The New York victory, which preserved the Liberty's 6–0 record at home, was largely due to Weatherspoon, who paced the team with 12 points and seven rebounds. "[When] she knocks down those shots, she gets in a rhythm," said Shock coach Nancy Lieberman-Cline. "There's nothing you can do."

From that win, however, the Liberty would spiral into a four-game slide, losing each game by a sizable margin. After the fourth loss, Coach Darsch came into the locker room before a game against Phoenix and handed each of her players a stick. After breaking her own stick, Darsch gathered the sticks again and tried to break them all at once—she couldn't. The Liberty players got the message; with everyone playing together, nothing could break them.

Darsch's demonstration apparently worked, as her Liberty won their next six games by an average of 15 points. The run culminated in an 85–67 romp over the Eastern Conference-leading Charlotte Sting. Vickie Johnson led the charge, hitting a trio of three-point bombs during a 22–0 first-half run. "Over the last six games, we have really come together as a team," Lobo said.

The Sting avenged the loss three nights later, but it seemed that nothing could stop the Liberty, who reeled off four more wins in another impressive homestand. After obliterating the Washington Mystics behind Kisha Ford's 19-point showing, the Liberty welcomed the defending champion Houston Comets to Madison Square Garden on August 15. More than 19,500 fans—the largest crowd to ever see a women's game in the Garden—watched New York destroy the Comets 70–54 for the first time in five tries.

After winning 10 of their last 11 games and blowing out the powerhouse from Houston, the Liberty seemed to have the momentum they needed to run to the league title. But then things

1998 DRAFT PICK ALBENA

BRANZOVA (ABOVE);

FORWARD KISHA

FORD (BOTTOM)

fell apart in the season's final two contests. The Liberty, needing to win just one of two games to secure a playoff spot, welcomed the Cleveland Rockers to the unfriendly confines of the Garden. With 17 seconds left in a tight game, Witherspoon was hit on the wrist going to the basket, but no foul was called, and Cleveland hung on to capture the game and the Eastern Conference title.

Despite the frustrating loss, New York still had the opportunity to claim a playoff spot two nights later with a win in Detroit. The upstart Shock, however, played the spoiler role, toppling the Liberty and their championship dreams 82–68. A determined Witherspoon led the charge with a team season-high 26 points, but an early 14-point Liberty lead evaporated. "It's frustrating," Darsch said sadly. "We haven't played the last two games like we did our past 10 or 11 games. . . . The emotion was there, but the energy was not."

RELOADING FOR '99

Despite the Liberty's disappointing finish in 1998, few could argue with the impressive performances put forth by the New York squad. Weatherspoon, the piston that drove the team once again, earned Defensive Player of the Year and All-WNBA

FORWARD VICKIE JOHNSON

Second-Team honors for the second time. T-Spoon also ranked among the league's "iron women," playing more than 33 minutes per game. In fact, New York's entire lineup seemed indestructible, with its starting five taking the floor to start all 30 games.

On top of their durability, the Liberty proved to be one of the most unforgiving defenses in the league, ranking second in fewest points-per-game allowed. With their aggressive defense keeping games close, the Liberty demonstrated a knack for coming out on top in tight contests, going 5–0 in overtime over the two seasons and posting a 6–1 mark in 1998 games decided by four points or less.

With Weatherspoon spearheading New York's renowned defense, the other "Spoon" led the offensive charge once again. Witherspoon was quietly one of the league's most lethal shooters, netting nearly 14 points per game, while Lobo—the team's premiere rebounder—Hampton, and Johnson each averaged between nine and 13 points per game. "We had great team chemistry," Blazejowski summarized. "When we ran, we could run with anyone. This was an exciting team."

Unfortunately for Coach Darsch, excitement did not compensate for the franchise's two playoff-eliminating losses at the end of the season. Darsch was let go, and the Liberty put their faith in new head coach Richie Audubato, a basketball mind with 19 years of sidelines experience in the NBA. Audubato, a New Jersey native, welcomed the new challenge and environment provided in New York. "Over the past two seasons," he said, "I've watched the growth and enormous success of the WNBA, and I'm excited to be a part of one of the league's preeminent franchises."

With offensive threat Vanessa Nygaard healthy and added to New York's already dangerous arsenal in 1999, the Liberty promise to remain among the league's heavyweights. With new leadership and the loyal support of the Big Apple, the Liberty should stand as tall as their namesake for years to come.